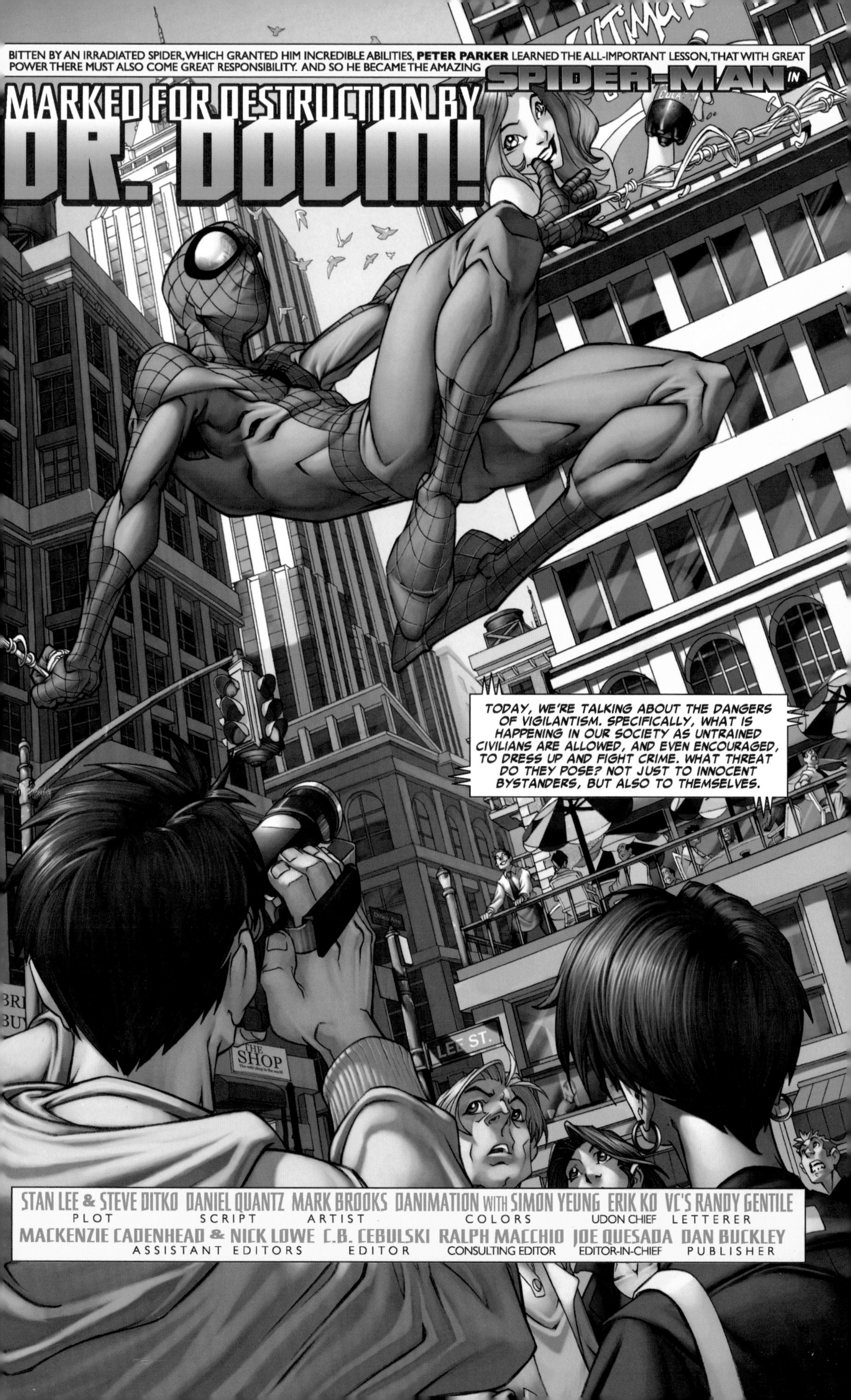

BITTEN BY AN IRRADIATED SPIDER, WHICH GRANTED HIM INCREDIBLE ABILITIES, PETER PARKER LEARNED THE ALL-IMPORTANT LESSON, THAT WITH GREAT POWER THERE MUST ALSO COME GREAT RESPONSIBILITY. AND SO HE BECAME THE AMAZING SPIDER-MAN IN
MARKED FOR DESTRUCTION BY DR. DOOM!
TODAY, WE'RE TALKING ABOUT THE DANGERS OF VIGILANTISM. SPECIFICALLY, WHAT IS HAPPENING IN OUR SOCIETY AS UNTRAINED CIVILIANS ARE ALLOWED, AND EVEN ENCOURAGED, TO DRESS UP AND FIGHT CRIME. WHAT THREAT DO THEY POSE? NOT JUST TO INNOCENT BYSTANDERS, BUT ALSO TO THEMSELVES.
LEE ST.
THE SHOP
STAN LEE & STEVE DITKO PLOT
DANIEL QUANTZ SCRIPT
MARK BROOKS ARTIST
DANIMATION WITH SIMON YEUNG COLORS
ERIK KO UDON CHIEF
VC'S RANDY GENTILE LETTERER
MACKENZIE CADENHEAD & NICK LOWE ASSISTANT EDITORS
C.B. CEBULSKI EDITOR
RALPH MACCHIO CONSULTING EDITOR
JOE QUESADA EDITOR-IN-CHIEF
DAN BUCKLEY PUBLISHER

VISIT US AT
www.abdopub.com

Spotlight, a division of ABDO Publishing Company Inc., is the school and library distributor of the Marvel Entertainment books.

Library bound edition © 2006

Library of Congress Cataloging-in-Publication Data

Marked For Destruction By Dr. Doom!

ISBN 1-59961-015-9   (Reinforced Library Bound Edition)

All Spotlight books are reinforced library binding and manufactured in the United States of America

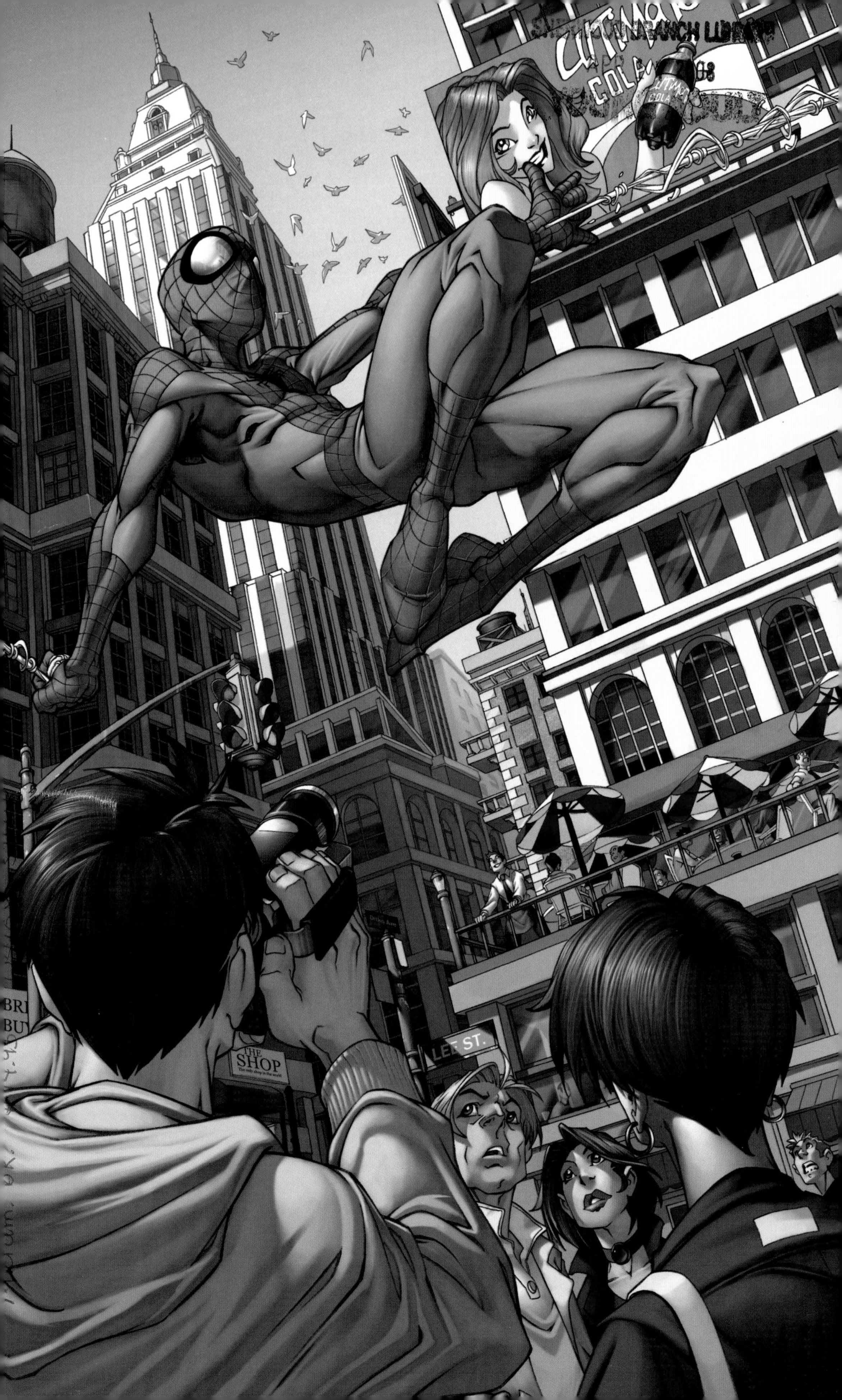
COLA
THE SHOP
The only shop in the world
ST.

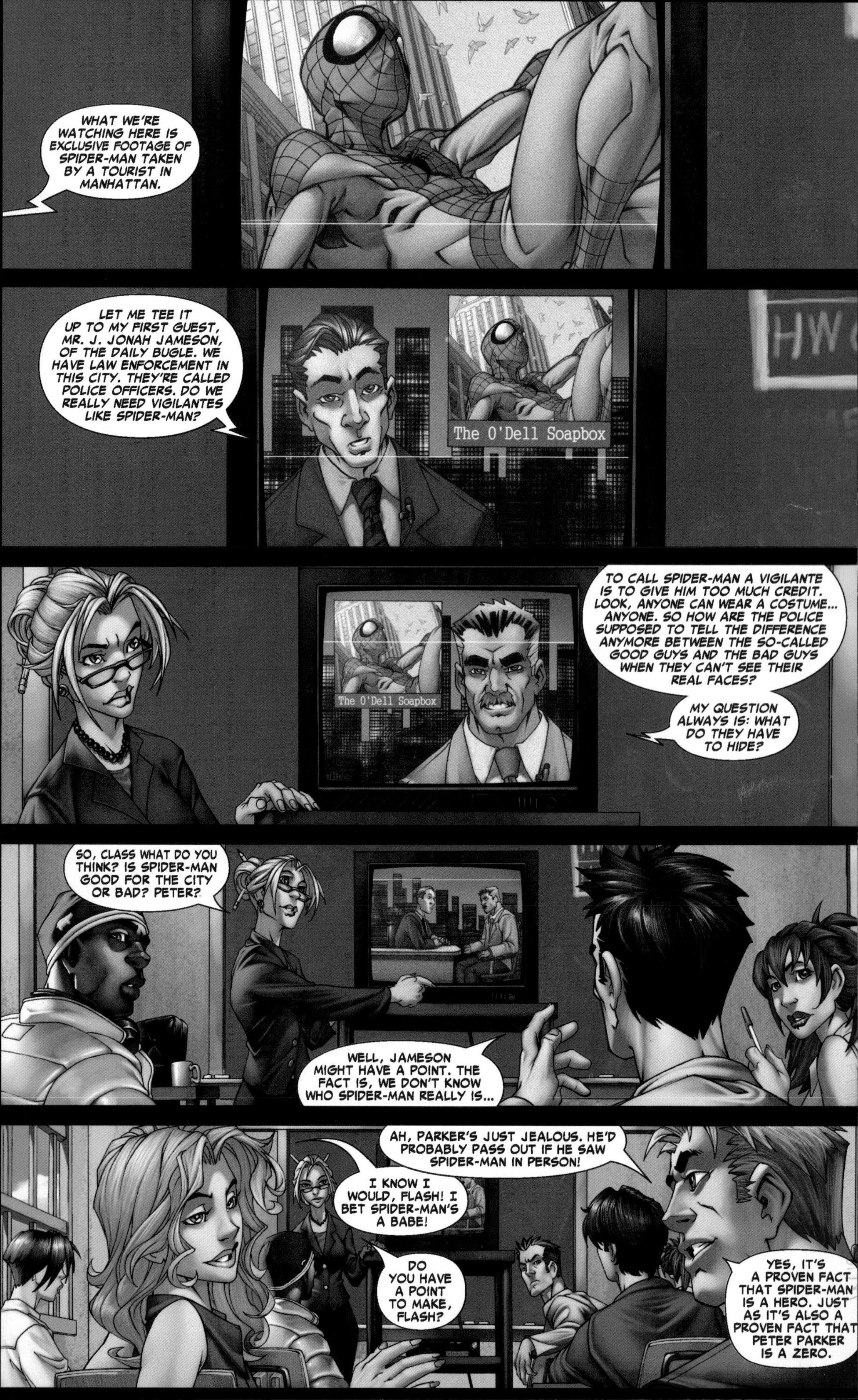
WHAT WE'RE WATCHING HERE IS EXCLUSIVE FOOTAGE OF SPIDER-MAN TAKEN BY A TOURIST IN MANHATTAN.
LET ME TEE IT UP TO MY FIRST GUEST, MR. J. JONAH JAMESON, OF THE DAILY BUGLE. WE HAVE LAW ENFORCEMENT IN THIS CITY. THEY'RE CALLED POLICE OFFICERS. DO WE REALLY NEED VIGILANTES LIKE SPIDER-MAN?
The O'Dell Soapbox
The O'Dell Soapbox
TO CALL SPIDER-MAN A VIGILANTE IS TO GIVE HIM TOO MUCH CREDIT. LOOK, ANYONE CAN WEAR A COSTUME... ANYONE. SO HOW ARE THE POLICE SUPPOSED TO TELL THE DIFFERENCE ANYMORE BETWEEN THE SO-CALLED GOOD GUYS AND THE BAD GUYS WHEN THEY CAN'T SEE THEIR REAL FACES?
MY QUESTION ALWAYS IS: WHAT DO THEY HAVE TO HIDE?
SO, CLASS WHAT DO YOU THINK? IS SPIDER-MAN GOOD FOR THE CITY OR BAD? PETER?
WELL, JAMESON MIGHT HAVE A POINT. THE FACT IS, WE DON'T KNOW WHO SPIDER-MAN REALLY IS...
AH, PARKER'S JUST JEALOUS. HE'D PROBABLY PASS OUT IF HE SAW SPIDER-MAN IN PERSON!
I KNOW I WOULD, FLASH! I BET SPIDER-MAN'S A BABE!
DO YOU HAVE A POINT TO MAKE, FLASH?
YES, IT'S A PROVEN FACT THAT SPIDER-MAN IS A HERO. JUST AS IT'S ALSO A PROVEN FACT THAT PETER PARKER IS A ZERO.

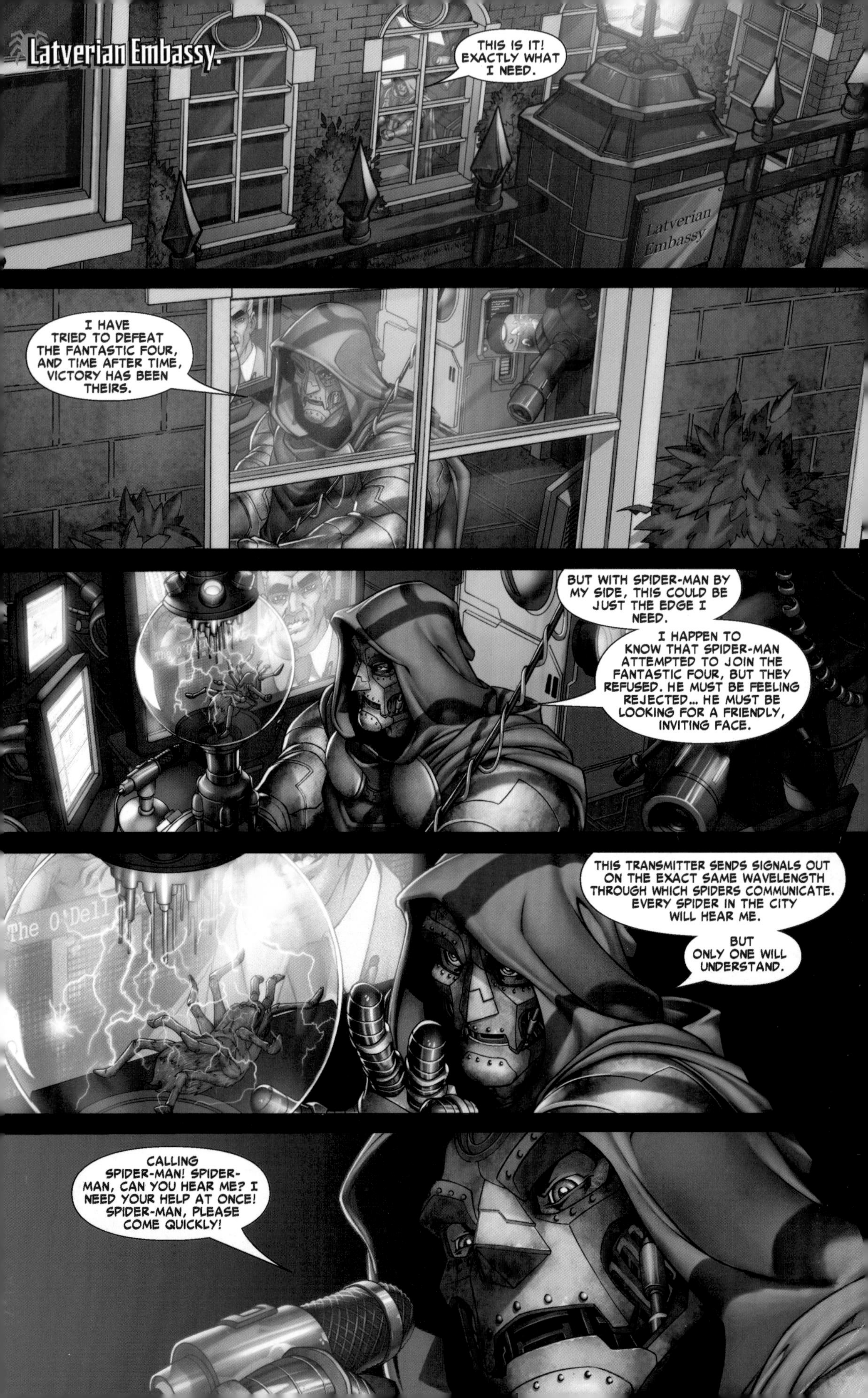
Latverian Embassy.
THIS IS IT! EXACTLY WHAT I NEED.
Latverian Embassy
I HAVE TRIED TO DEFEAT THE FANTASTIC FOUR, AND TIME AFTER TIME, VICTORY HAS BEEN THEIRS.
BUT WITH SPIDER-MAN BY MY SIDE, THIS COULD BE JUST THE EDGE I NEED.
I HAPPEN TO KNOW THAT SPIDER-MAN ATTEMPTED TO JOIN THE FANTASTIC FOUR, BUT THEY REFUSED. HE MUST BE FEELING REJECTED... HE MUST BE LOOKING FOR A FRIENDLY, INVITING FACE.
THIS TRANSMITTER SENDS SIGNALS OUT ON THE EXACT SAME WAVELENGTH THROUGH WHICH SPIDERS COMMUNICATE. EVERY SPIDER IN THE CITY WILL HEAR ME.
BUT ONLY ONE WILL UNDERSTAND.
CALLING SPIDER-MAN! SPIDER-MAN, CAN YOU HEAR ME? I NEED YOUR HELP AT ONCE! SPIDER-MAN, PLEASE COME QUICKLY!

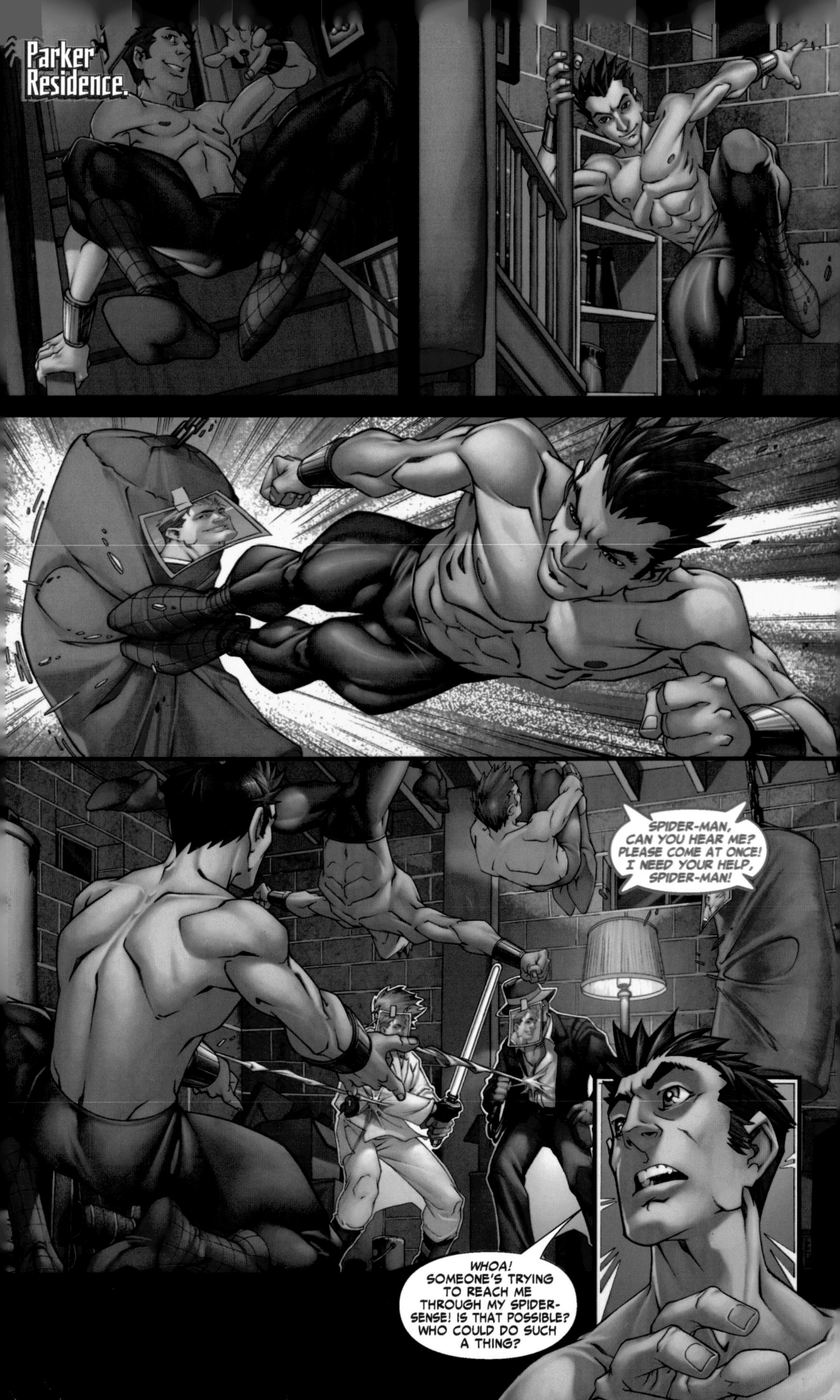
Parker Residence.
SPIDER-MAN, CAN YOU HEAR ME? PLEASE COME AT ONCE! I NEED YOUR HELP, SPIDER-MAN!
WHOA! SOMEONE'S TRYING TO REACH ME THROUGH MY SPIDER-SENSE! IS THAT POSSIBLE? WHO COULD DO SUCH A THING?

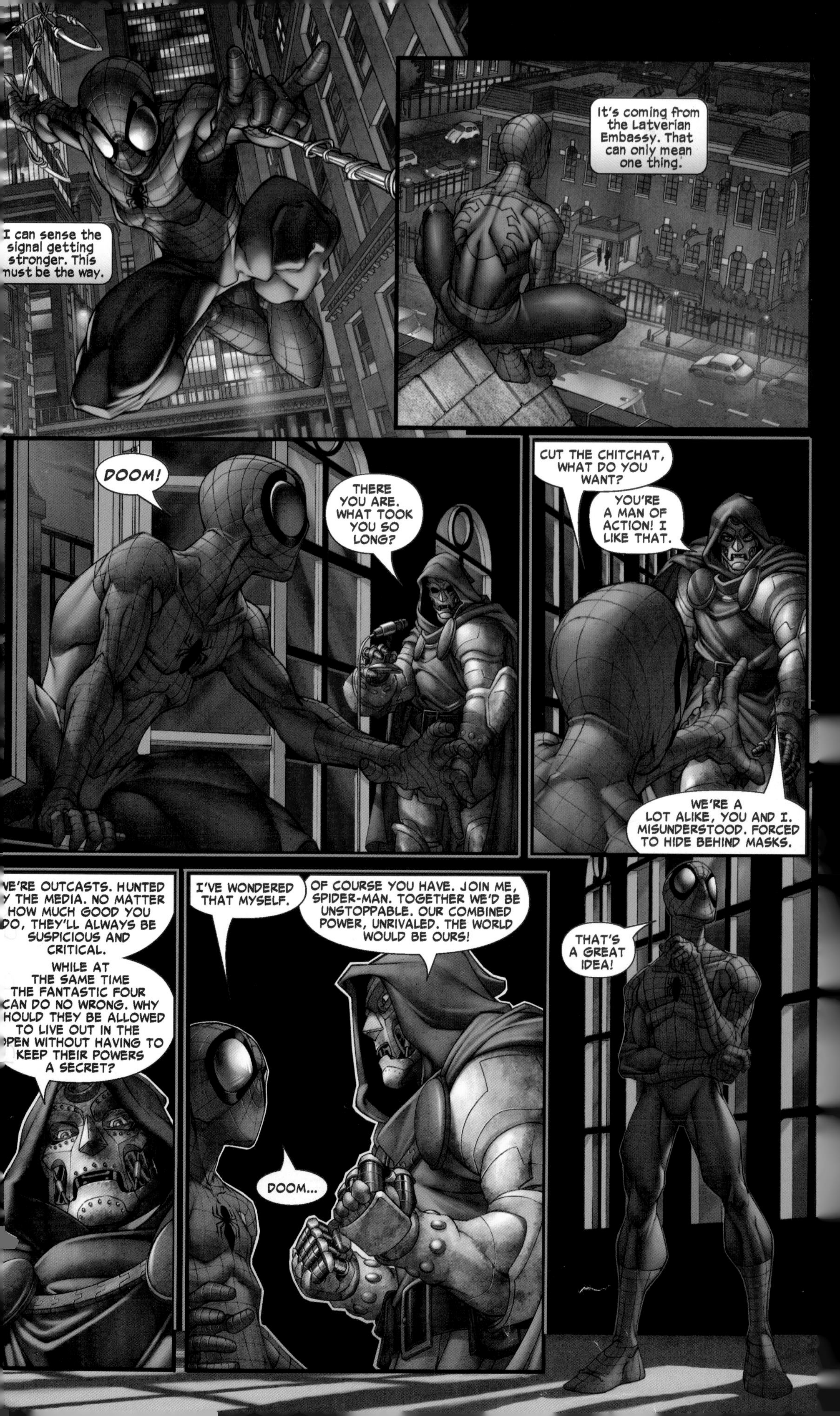
I can sense the signal getting stronger. This must be the way.
It's coming from the Latverian Embassy. That can only mean one thing.
DOOM!
THERE YOU ARE. WHAT TOOK YOU SO LONG?
CUT THE CHITCHAT, WHAT DO YOU WANT?
YOU'RE A MAN OF ACTION! I LIKE THAT.
WE'RE A LOT ALIKE, YOU AND I. MISUNDERSTOOD. FORCED TO HIDE BEHIND MASKS.
E'RE OUTCASTS. HUNTED Y THE MEDIA. NO MATTER HOW MUCH GOOD YOU DO, THEY'LL ALWAYS BE SUSPICIOUS AND CRITICAL.
WHILE AT THE SAME TIME THE FANTASTIC FOUR CAN DO NO WRONG. WHY HOULD THEY BE ALLOWED TO LIVE OUT IN THE PEN WITHOUT HAVING TO KEEP THEIR POWERS A SECRET?
I'VE WONDERED THAT MYSELF.
OF COURSE YOU HAVE. JOIN ME, SPIDER-MAN. TOGETHER WE'D BE UNSTOPPABLE. OUR COMBINED POWER, UNRIVALED. THE WORLD WOULD BE OURS!
DOOM...
THAT'S A GREAT IDEA!

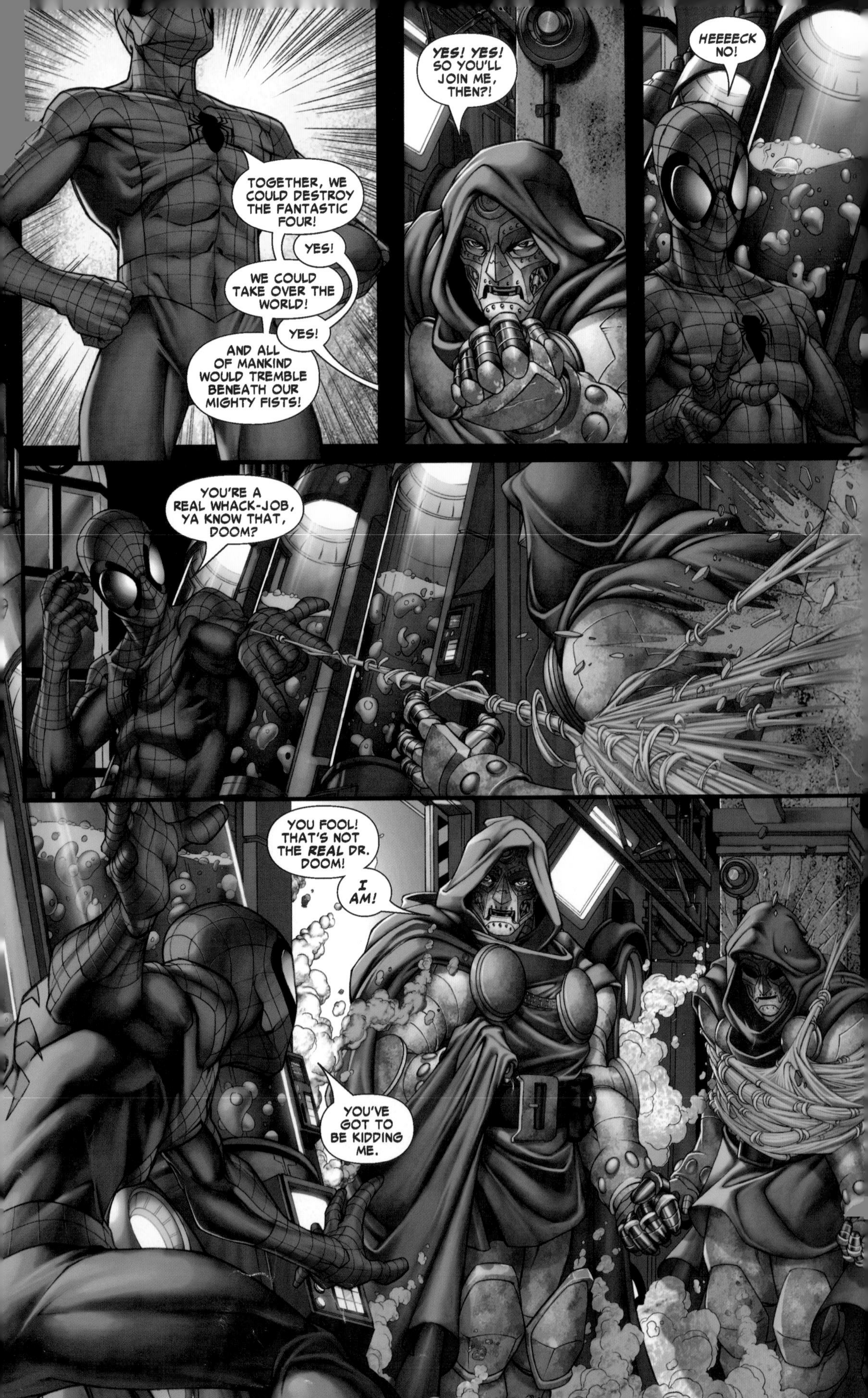
TOGETHER, WE COULD DESTROY THE FANTASTIC FOUR!
YES!
WE COULD TAKE OVER THE WORLD!
YES!
AND ALL OF MANKIND WOULD TREMBLE BENEATH OUR MIGHTY FISTS!
YES! YES! SO YOU'LL JOIN ME, THEN?!
HEEEECK NO!
YOU'RE A REAL WHACK-JOB, YA KNOW THAT, DOOM?
YOU FOOL! THAT'S NOT THE REAL DR. DOOM!
I AM!
YOU'VE GOT TO BE KIDDING ME.

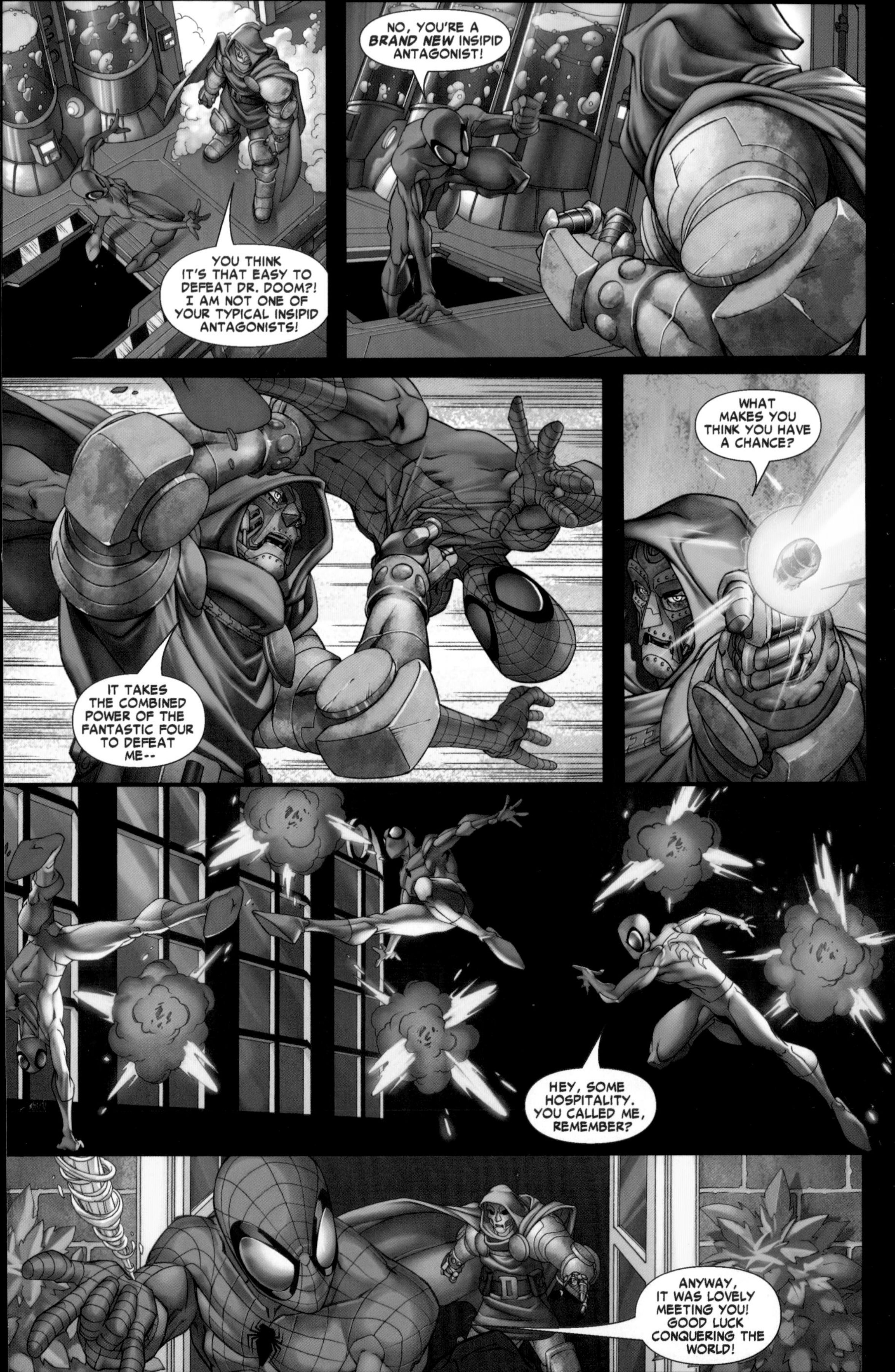
YOU THINK IT'S THAT EASY TO DEFEAT DR. DOOM?! I AM NOT ONE OF YOUR TYPICAL INSIPID ANTAGONISTS!
NO, YOU'RE A BRAND NEW INSIPID ANTAGONIST!
IT TAKES THE COMBINED POWER OF THE FANTASTIC FOUR TO DEFEAT ME--
WHAT MAKES YOU THINK YOU HAVE A CHANCE?
HEY, SOME HOSPITALITY. YOU CALLED ME, REMEMBER?
ANYWAY, IT WAS LOVELY MEETING YOU! GOOD LUCK CONQUERING THE WORLD!

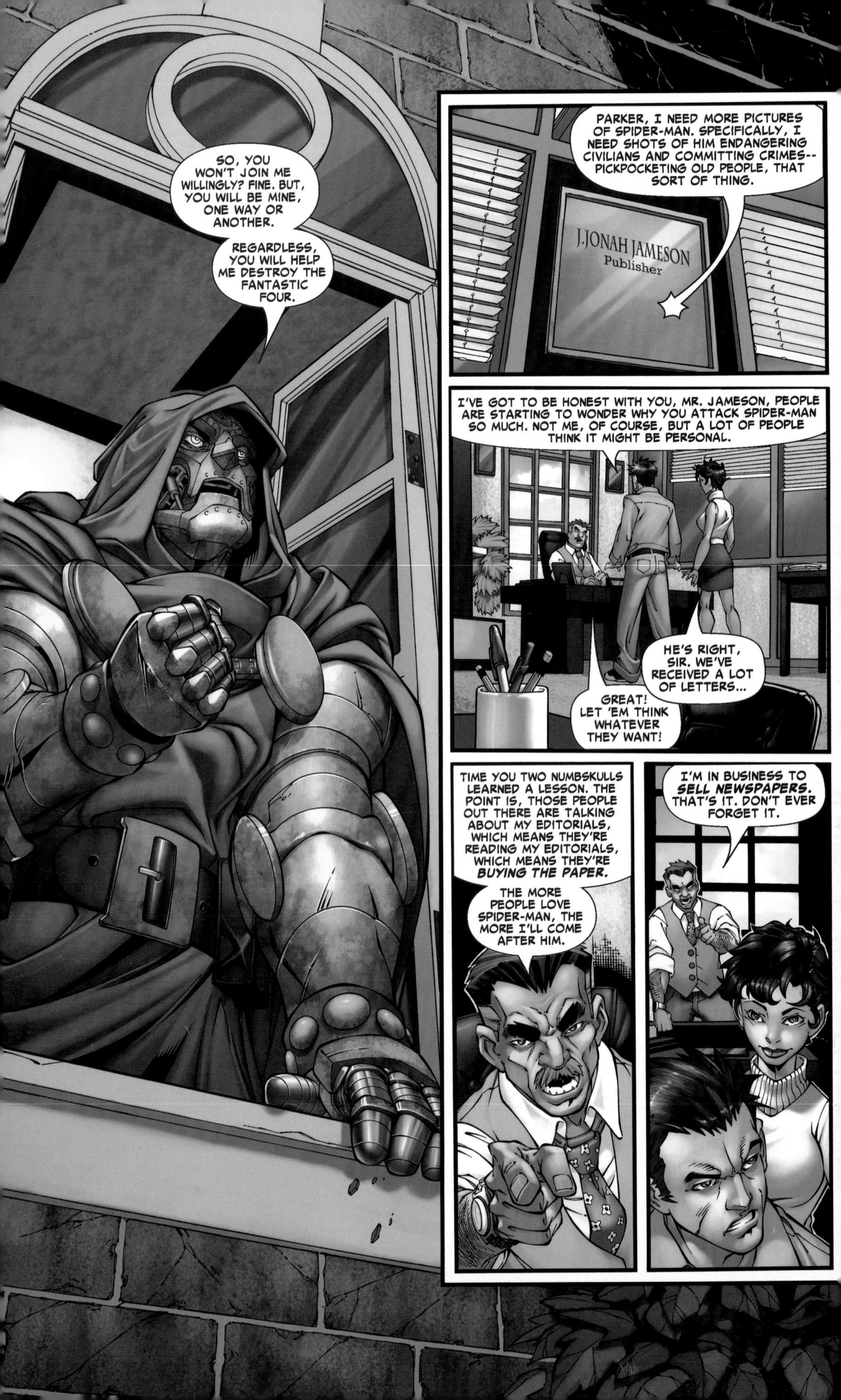
SO, YOU WON'T JOIN ME WILLINGLY? FINE. BUT, YOU WILL BE MINE, ONE WAY OR ANOTHER.
REGARDLESS, YOU WILL HELP ME DESTROY THE FANTASTIC FOUR.
PARKER, I NEED MORE PICTURES OF SPIDER-MAN. SPECIFICALLY, I NEED SHOTS OF HIM ENDANGERING CIVILIANS AND COMMITTING CRIMES-- PICKPOCKETING OLD PEOPLE, THAT SORT OF THING.
J.JONAH JAMESON
Publisher
I'VE GOT TO BE HONEST WITH YOU, MR. JAMESON, PEOPLE ARE STARTING TO WONDER WHY YOU ATTACK SPIDER-MAN SO MUCH. NOT ME, OF COURSE, BUT A LOT OF PEOPLE THINK IT MIGHT BE PERSONAL.
HE'S RIGHT, SIR. WE'VE RECEIVED A LOT OF LETTERS...
GREAT! LET 'EM THINK WHATEVER THEY WANT!
TIME YOU TWO NUMBSKULLS LEARNED A LESSON. THE POINT IS, THOSE PEOPLE OUT THERE ARE TALKING ABOUT MY EDITORIALS, WHICH MEANS THEY'RE READING MY EDITORIALS, WHICH MEANS THEY'RE *BUYING THE PAPER.*
THE MORE PEOPLE LOVE SPIDER-MAN, THE MORE I'LL COME AFTER HIM.
I'M IN BUSINESS TO *SELL NEWSPAPERS.* THAT'S IT. DON'T EVER FORGET IT.

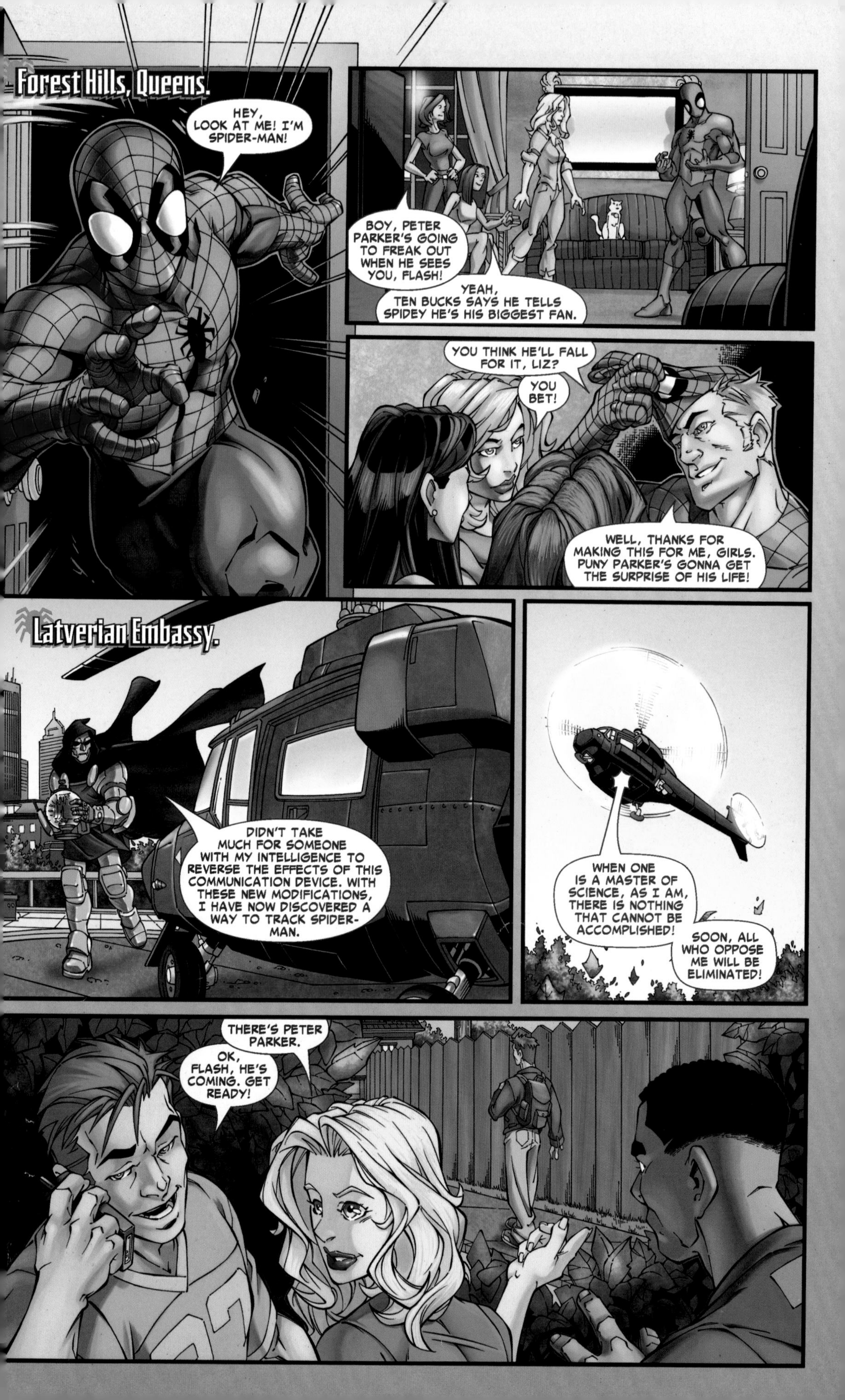
Forest Hills, Queens.
HEY, LOOK AT ME! I'M SPIDER-MAN!
BOY, PETER PARKER'S GOING TO FREAK OUT WHEN HE SEES YOU, FLASH!
YEAH, TEN BUCKS SAYS HE TELLS SPIDEY HE'S HIS BIGGEST FAN.
YOU THINK HE'LL FALL FOR IT, LIZ?
YOU BET!
WELL, THANKS FOR MAKING THIS FOR ME, GIRLS. PUNY PARKER'S GONNA GET THE SURPRISE OF HIS LIFE!
Latverian Embassy.
DIDN'T TAKE MUCH FOR SOMEONE WITH MY INTELLIGENCE TO REVERSE THE EFFECTS OF THIS COMMUNICATION DEVICE. WITH THESE NEW MODIFICATIONS, I HAVE NOW DISCOVERED A WAY TO TRACK SPIDER-MAN.
WHEN ONE IS A MASTER OF SCIENCE, AS I AM, THERE IS NOTHING THAT CANNOT BE ACCOMPLISHED!
SOON, ALL WHO OPPOSE ME WILL BE ELIMINATED!
THERE'S PETER PARKER.
OK, FLASH, HE'S COMING. GET READY!

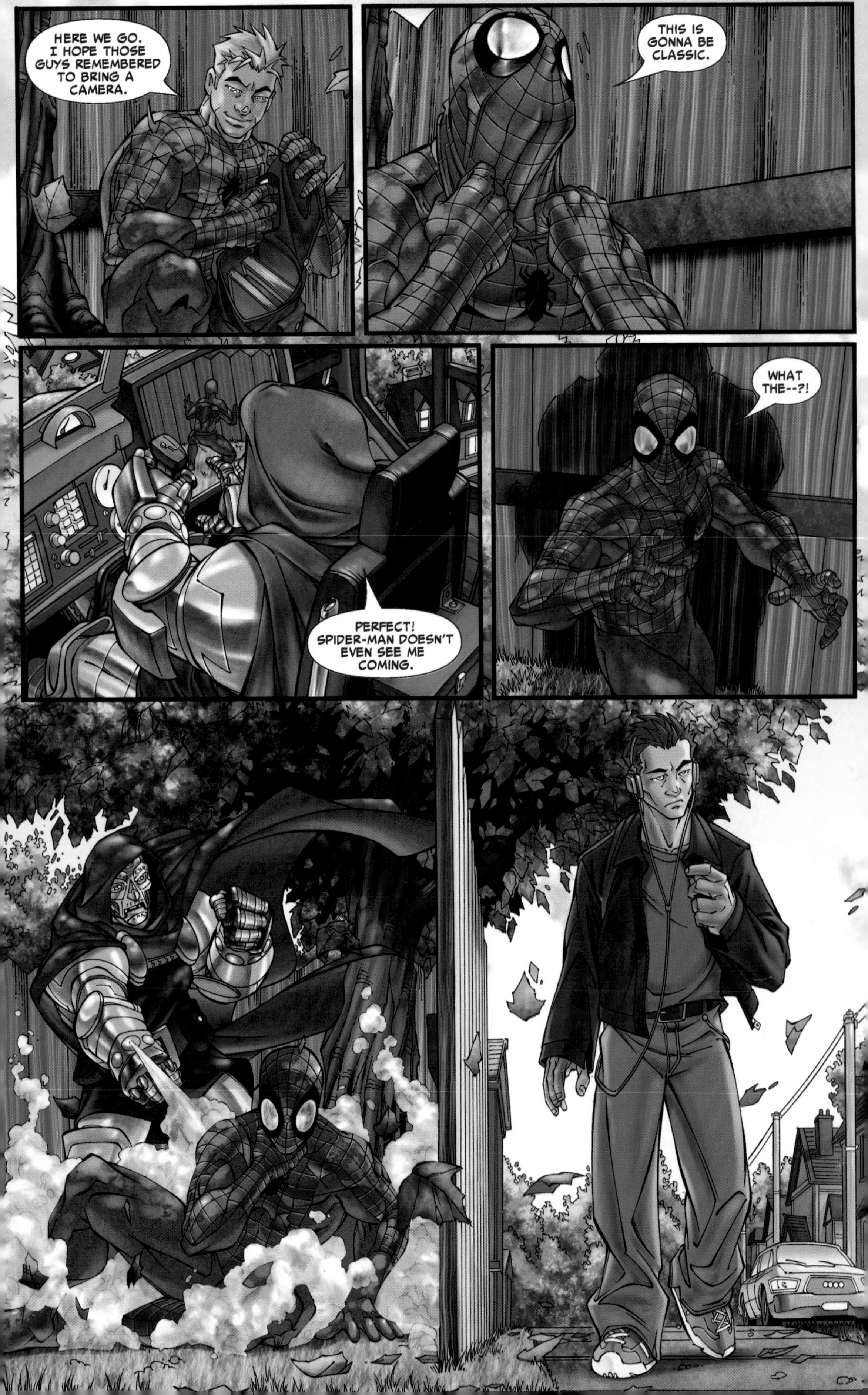
HERE WE GO. I HOPE THOSE GUYS REMEMBERED TO BRING A CAMERA.
THIS IS GONNA BE CLASSIC.
PERFECT! SPIDER-MAN DOESN'T EVEN SEE ME COMING.
WHAT THE--?!

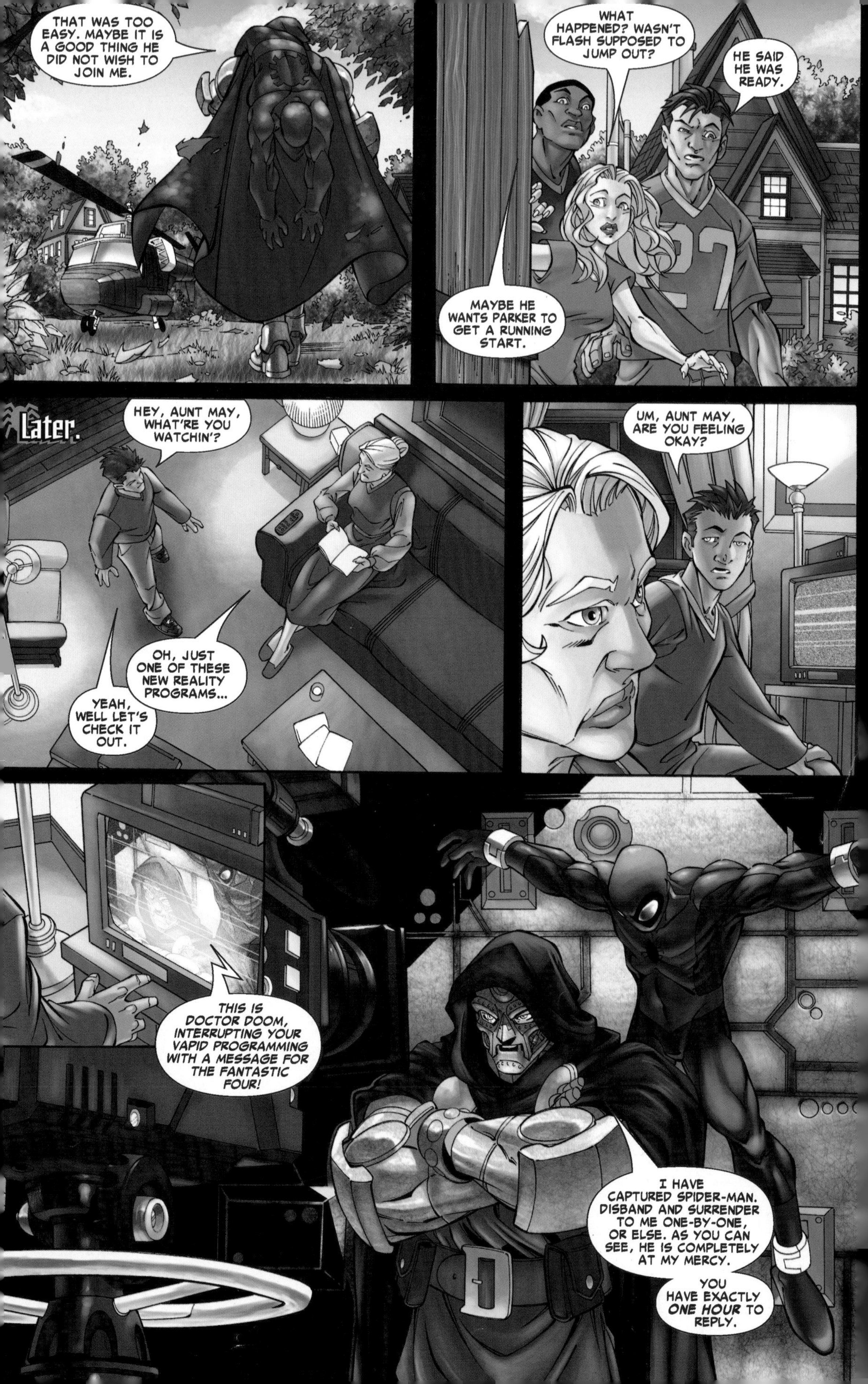
THAT WAS TOO EASY. MAYBE IT IS A GOOD THING HE DID NOT WISH TO JOIN ME.
WHAT HAPPENED? WASN'T FLASH SUPPOSED TO JUMP OUT?
HE SAID HE WAS READY.
MAYBE HE WANTS PARKER TO GET A RUNNING START.
Later.
HEY, AUNT MAY, WHAT'RE YOU WATCHIN'?
OH, JUST ONE OF THESE NEW REALITY PROGRAMS...
YEAH, WELL LET'S CHECK IT OUT.
UM, AUNT MAY, ARE YOU FEELING OKAY?
THIS IS DOCTOR DOOM, INTERRUPTING YOUR VAPID PROGRAMMING WITH A MESSAGE FOR THE FANTASTIC FOUR!
I HAVE CAPTURED SPIDER-MAN. DISBAND AND SURRENDER TO ME ONE-BY-ONE, OR ELSE. AS YOU CAN SEE, HE IS COMPLETELY AT MY MERCY.
YOU HAVE EXACTLY *ONE HOUR* TO REPLY.

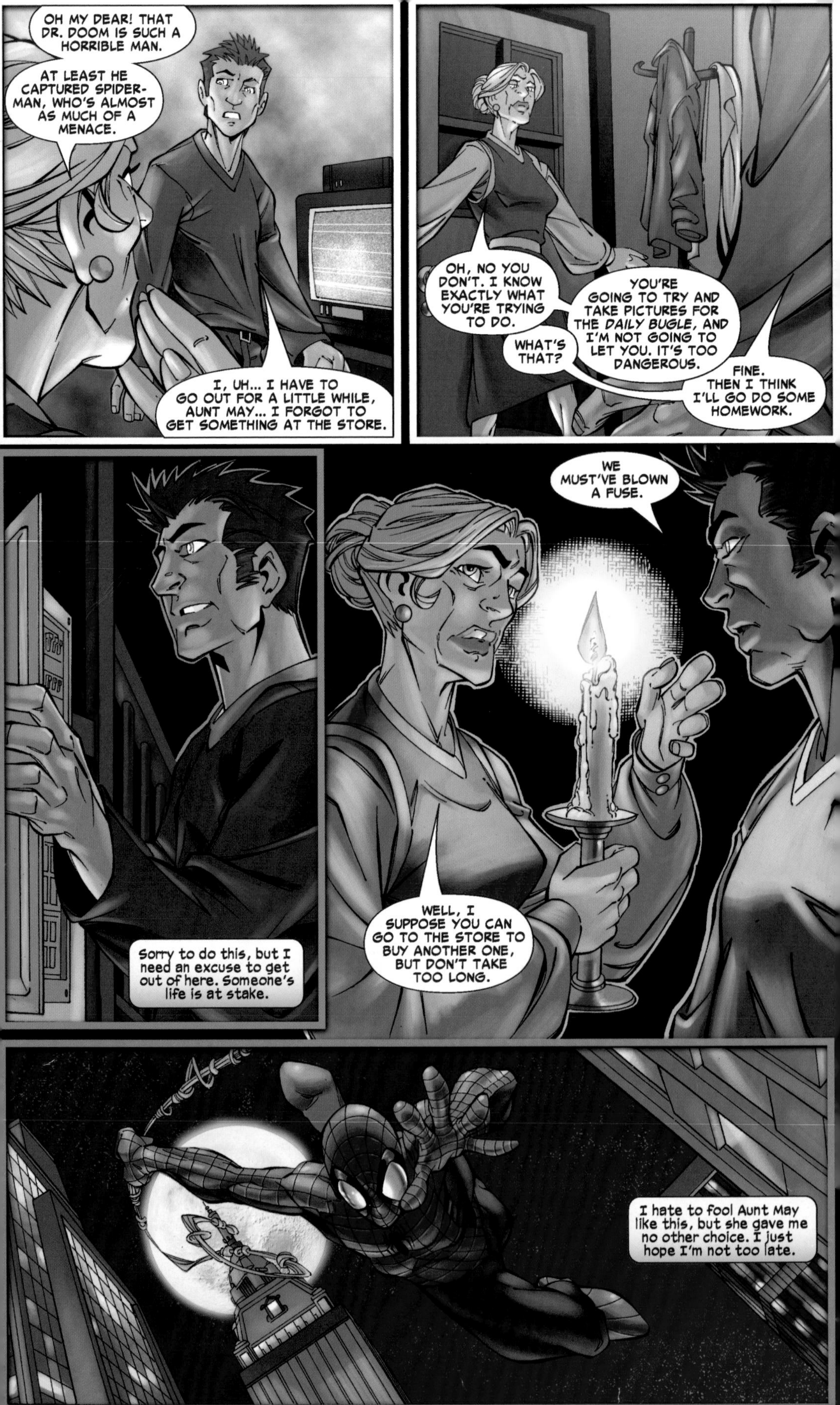
OH MY DEAR! THAT DR. DOOM IS SUCH A HORRIBLE MAN.
AT LEAST HE CAPTURED SPIDER-MAN, WHO'S ALMOST AS MUCH OF A MENACE.
I, UH... I HAVE TO GO OUT FOR A LITTLE WHILE, AUNT MAY... I FORGOT TO GET SOMETHING AT THE STORE.
OH, NO YOU DON'T. I KNOW EXACTLY WHAT YOU'RE TRYING TO DO.
WHAT'S THAT?
YOU'RE GOING TO TRY AND TAKE PICTURES FOR THE *DAILY BUGLE*, AND I'M NOT GOING TO LET YOU. IT'S TOO DANGEROUS.
FINE. THEN I THINK I'LL GO DO SOME HOMEWORK.
Sorry to do this, but I need an excuse to get out of here. Someone's life is at stake.
WE MUST'VE BLOWN A FUSE.
WELL, I SUPPOSE YOU CAN GO TO THE STORE TO BUY ANOTHER ONE, BUT DON'T TAKE TOO LONG.
I hate to fool Aunt May like this, but she gave me no other choice. I just hope I'm not too late.

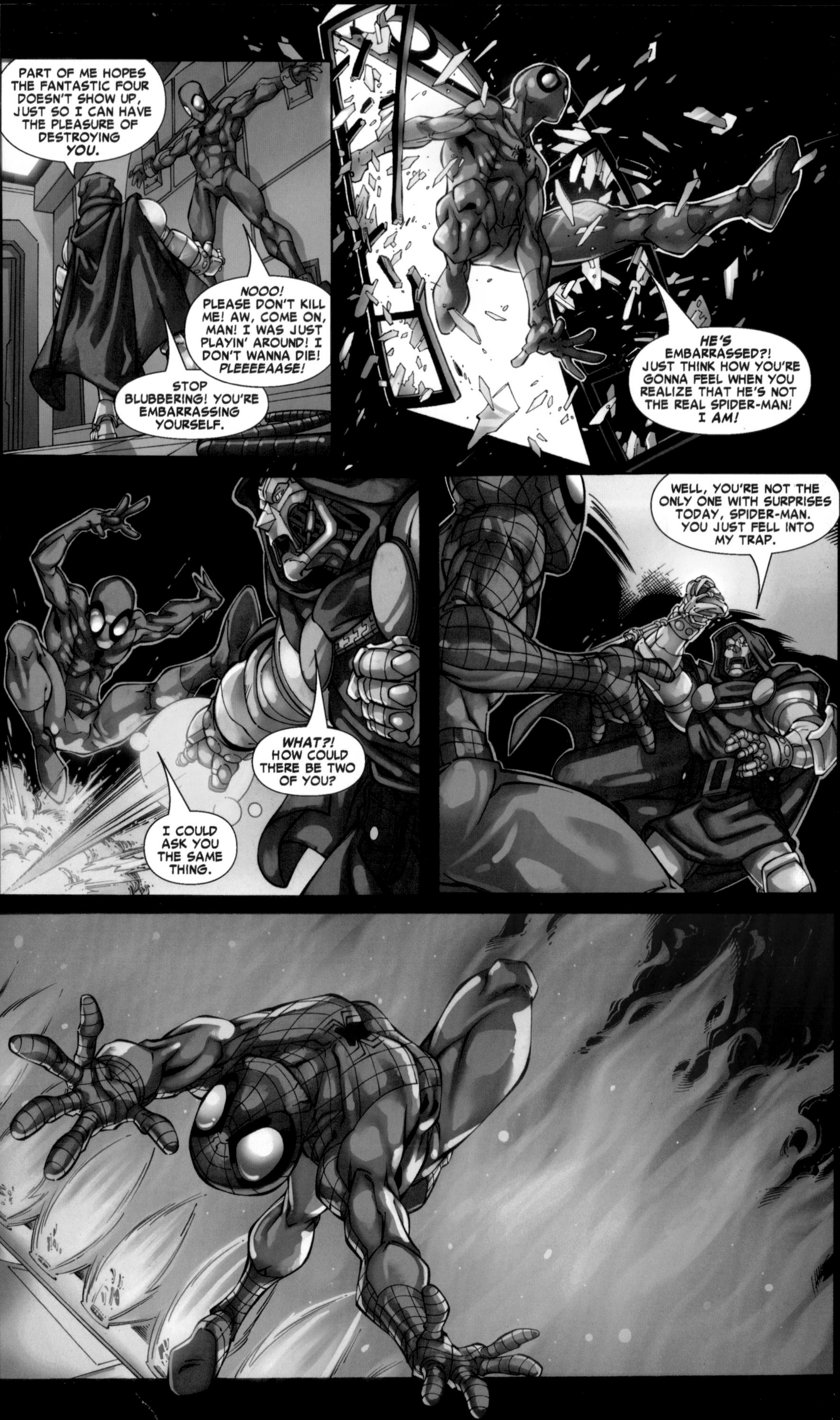
PART OF ME HOPES THE FANTASTIC FOUR DOESN'T SHOW UP, JUST SO I CAN HAVE THE PLEASURE OF DESTROYING YOU.
NOOO! PLEASE DON'T KILL ME! AW, COME ON, MAN! I WAS JUST PLAYIN' AROUND! I DON'T WANNA DIE! PLEEEEAASE!
STOP BLUBBERING! YOU'RE EMBARRASSING YOURSELF.
HE'S EMBARRASSED?! JUST THINK HOW YOU'RE GONNA FEEL WHEN YOU REALIZE THAT HE'S NOT THE REAL SPIDER-MAN! I AM!
WHAT?! HOW COULD THERE BE TWO OF YOU?
I COULD ASK YOU THE SAME THING.
WELL, YOU'RE NOT THE ONLY ONE WITH SURPRISES TODAY, SPIDER-MAN. YOU JUST FELL INTO MY TRAP.

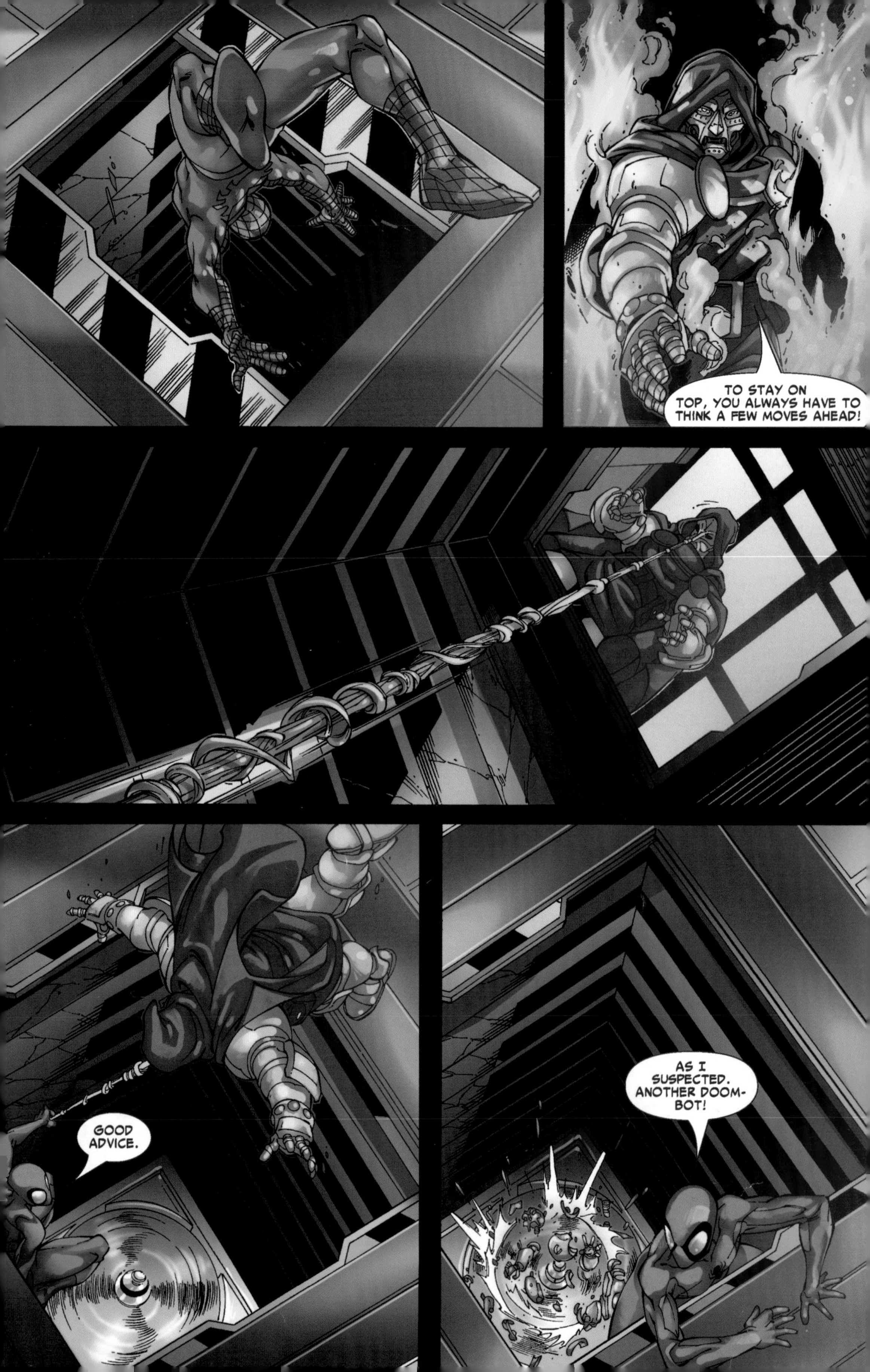
TO STAY ON TOP, YOU ALWAYS HAVE TO THINK A FEW MOVES AHEAD!
GOOD ADVICE.
AS I SUSPECTED. ANOTHER DOOM-BOT!

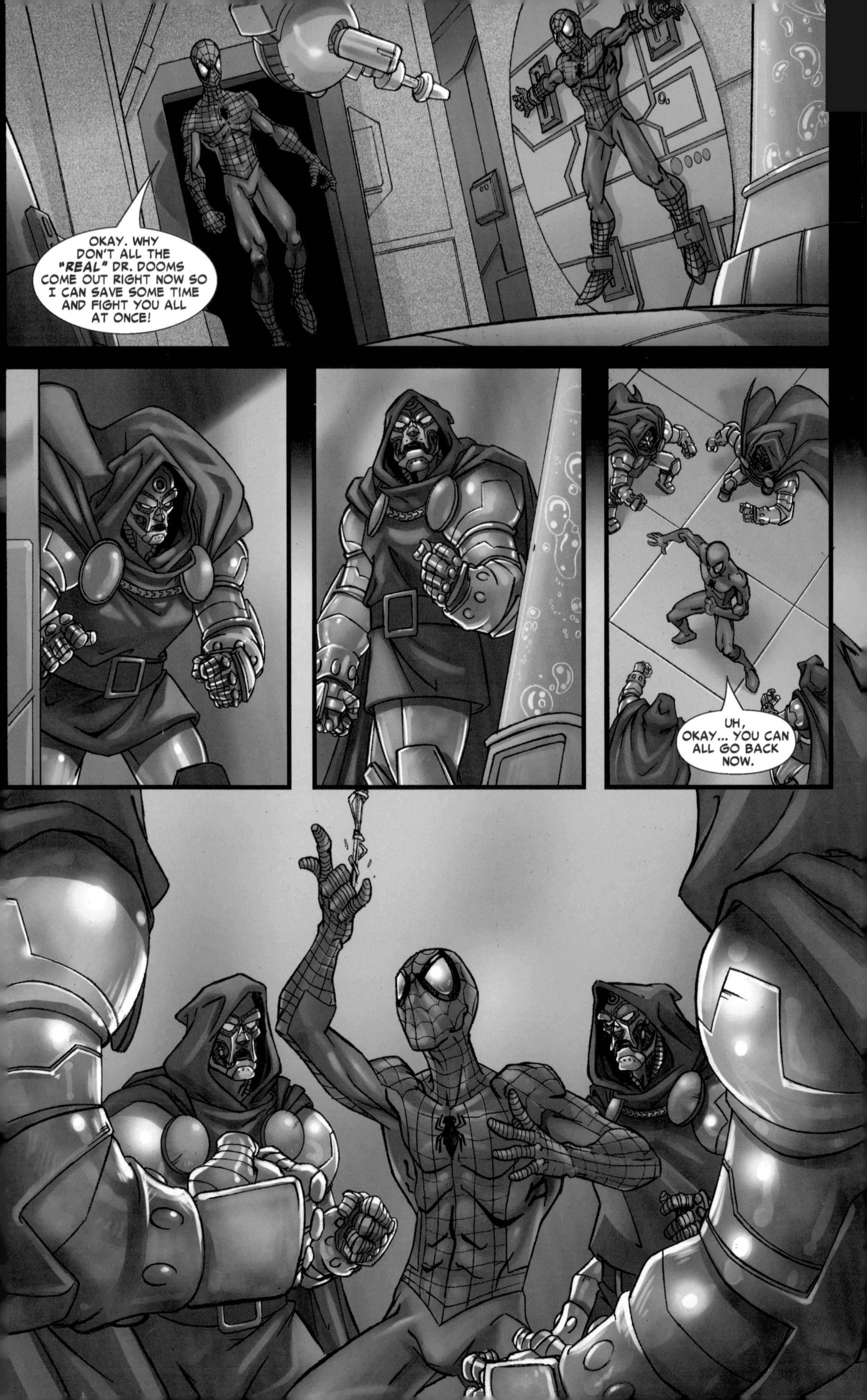
OKAY. WHY DON'T ALL THE "REAL" DR. DOOMS COME OUT RIGHT NOW SO I CAN SAVE SOME TIME AND FIGHT YOU ALL AT ONCE!
UH, OKAY... YOU CAN ALL GO BACK NOW.

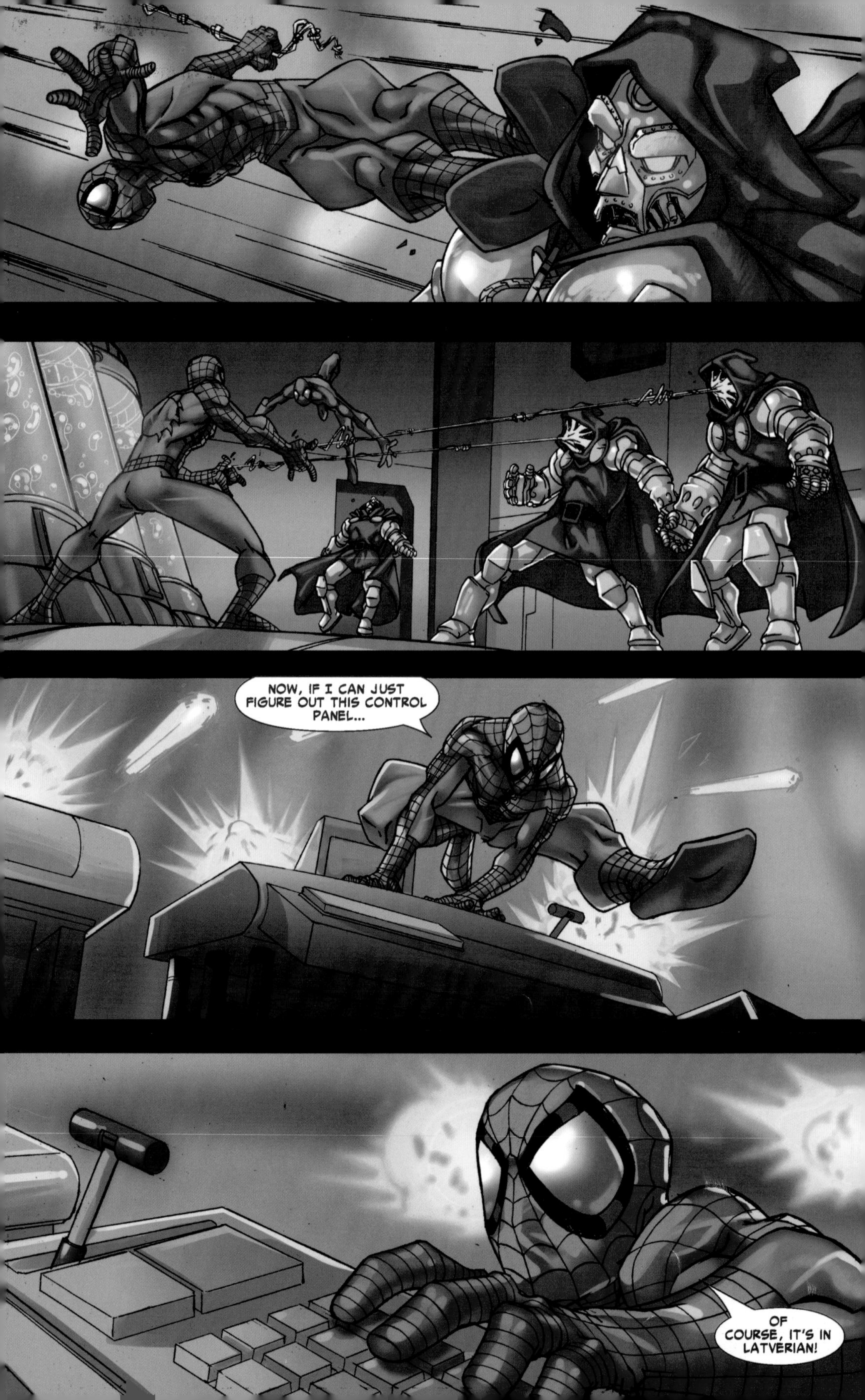
NOW, IF I CAN JUST FIGURE OUT THIS CONTROL PANEL...
OF COURSE, IT'S IN LATVERIAN!

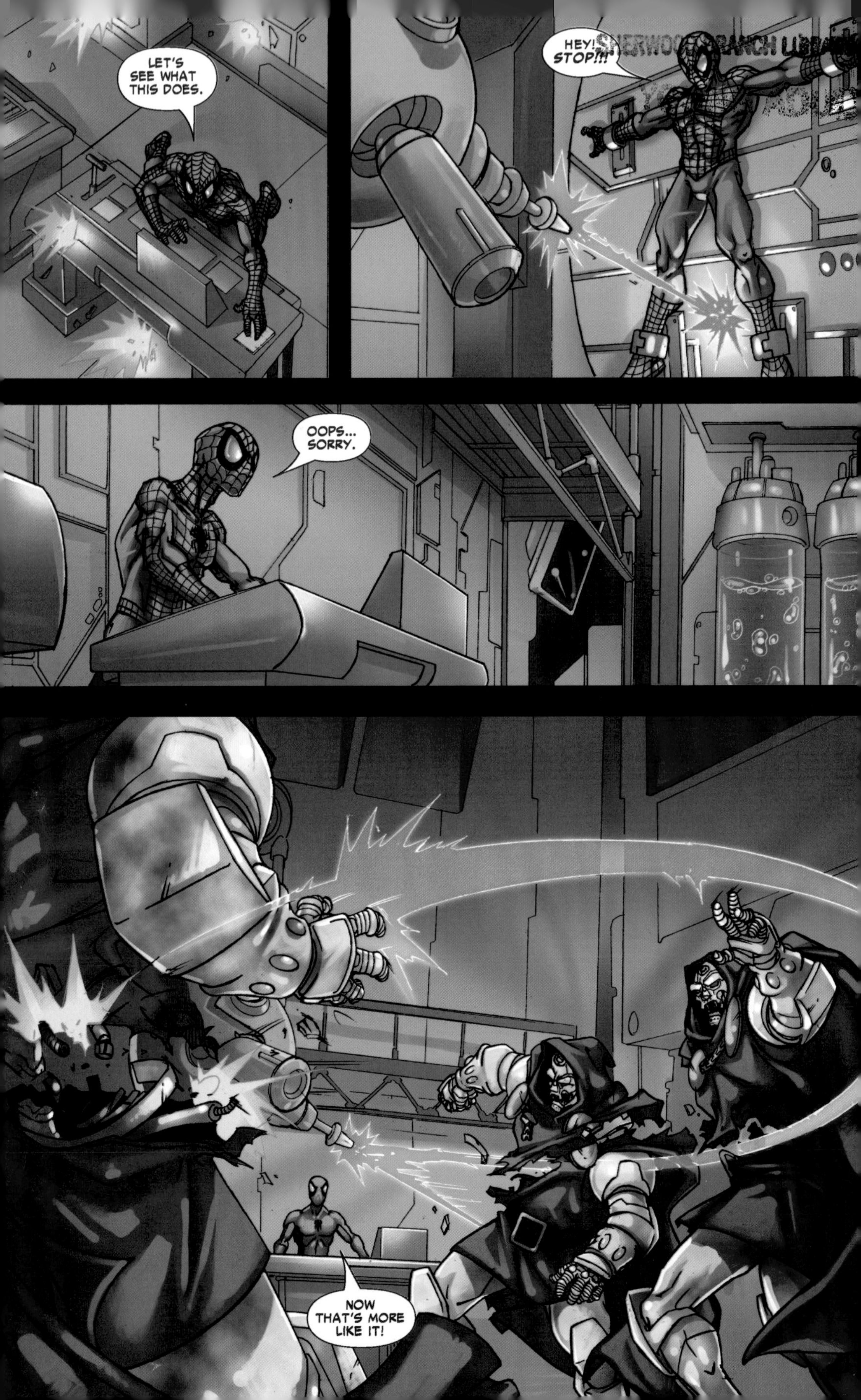
LET'S SEE WHAT THIS DOES.
HEY! STOP!!!
OOPS... SORRY.
NOW THAT'S MORE LIKE IT!

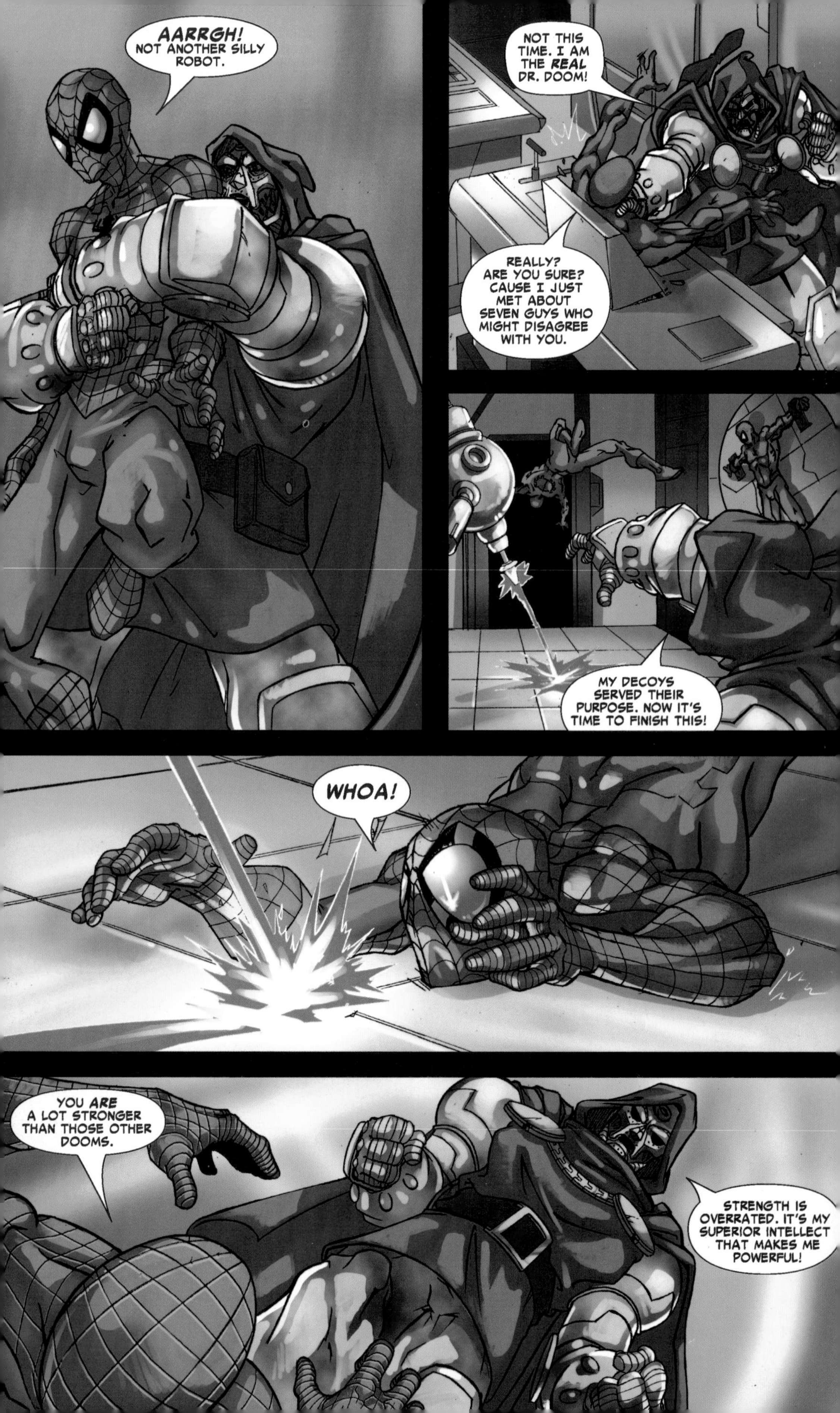
AARRGH!
NOT ANOTHER SILLY ROBOT.
NOT THIS TIME. I AM THE REAL DR. DOOM!
REALLY? ARE YOU SURE? CAUSE I JUST MET ABOUT SEVEN GUYS WHO MIGHT DISAGREE WITH YOU.
MY DECOYS SERVED THEIR PURPOSE. NOW IT'S TIME TO FINISH THIS!
WHOA!
YOU ARE A LOT STRONGER THAN THOSE OTHER DOOMS.
STRENGTH IS OVERRATED. IT'S MY SUPERIOR INTELLECT THAT MAKES ME POWERFUL!

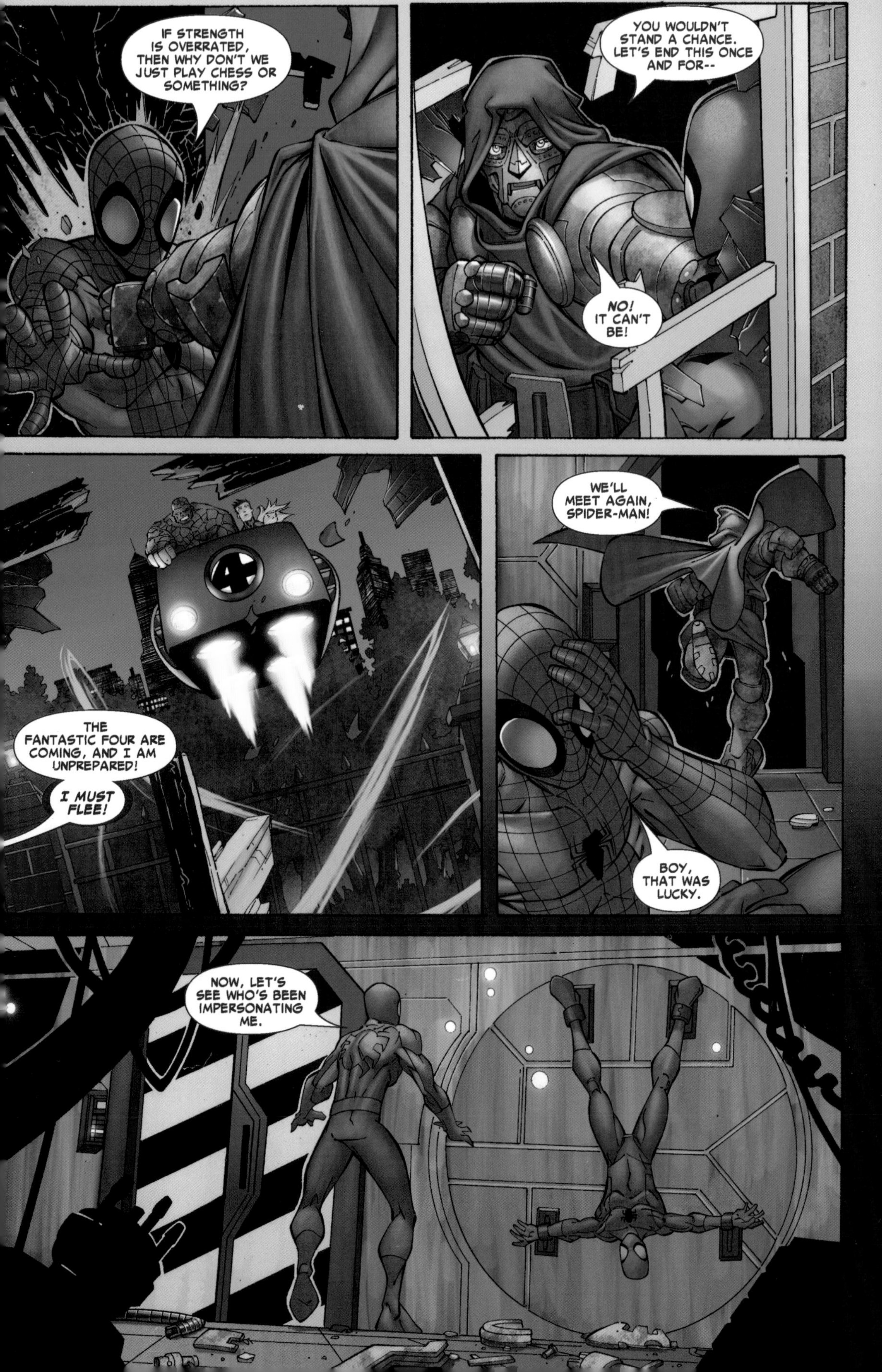
IF STRENGTH IS OVERRATED, THEN WHY DON'T WE JUST PLAY CHESS OR SOMETHING?
YOU WOULDN'T STAND A CHANCE. LET'S END THIS ONCE AND FOR--
NO! IT CAN'T BE!
THE FANTASTIC FOUR ARE COMING, AND I AM UNPREPARED!
I MUST FLEE!
WE'LL MEET AGAIN, SPIDER-MAN!
BOY, THAT WAS LUCKY.
NOW, LET'S SEE WHO'S BEEN IMPERSONATING ME.

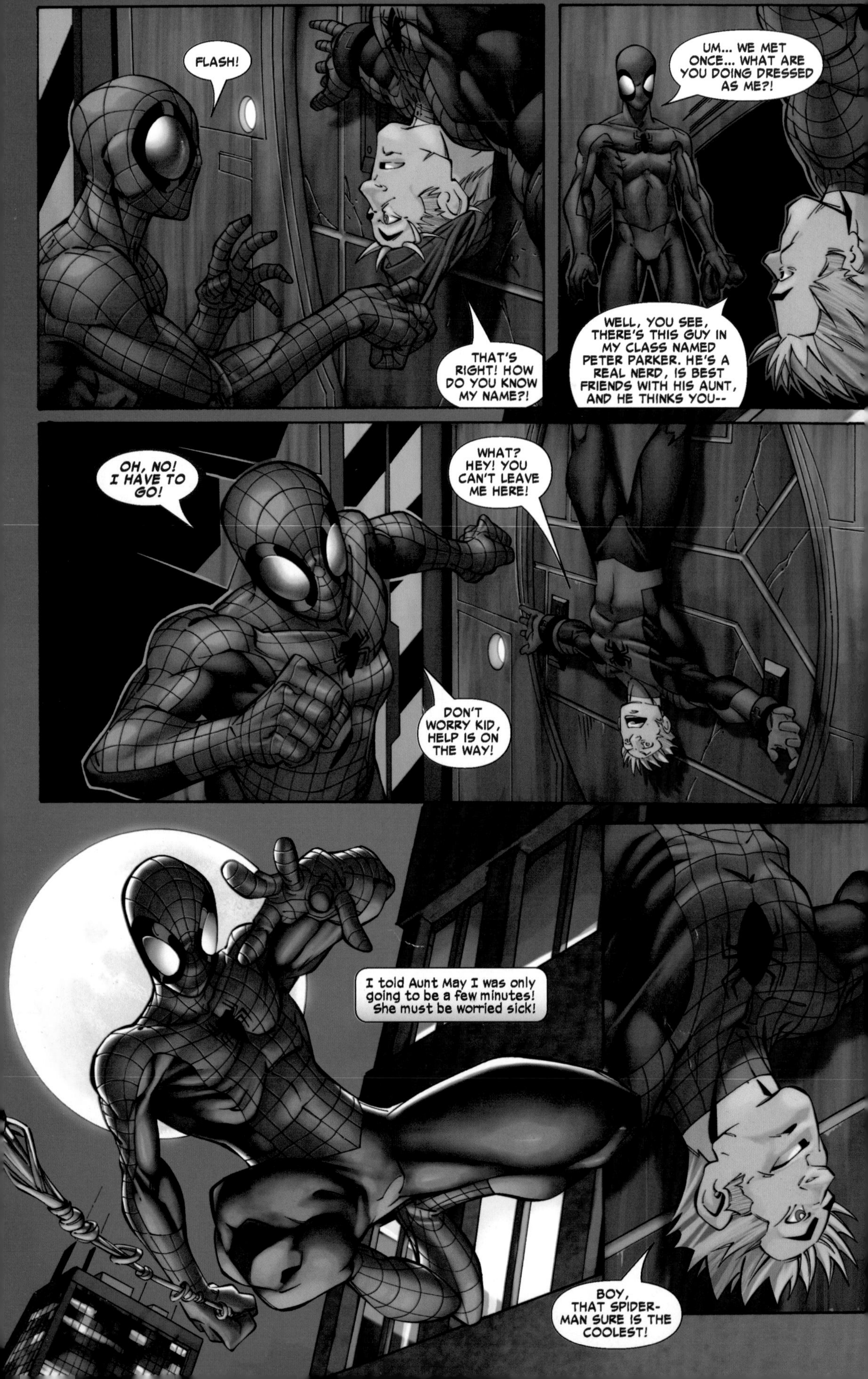
FLASH!
THAT'S RIGHT! HOW DO YOU KNOW MY NAME?!
UM... WE MET ONCE... WHAT ARE YOU DOING DRESSED AS ME?!
WELL, YOU SEE, THERE'S THIS GUY IN MY CLASS NAMED PETER PARKER. HE'S A REAL NERD, IS BEST FRIENDS WITH HIS AUNT, AND HE THINKS YOU--
OH, NO! I HAVE TO GO!
WHAT? HEY! YOU CAN'T LEAVE ME HERE!
DON'T WORRY KID, HELP IS ON THE WAY!
I told Aunt May I was only going to be a few minutes! She must be worried sick!
BOY, THAT SPIDER-MAN SURE IS THE COOLEST!

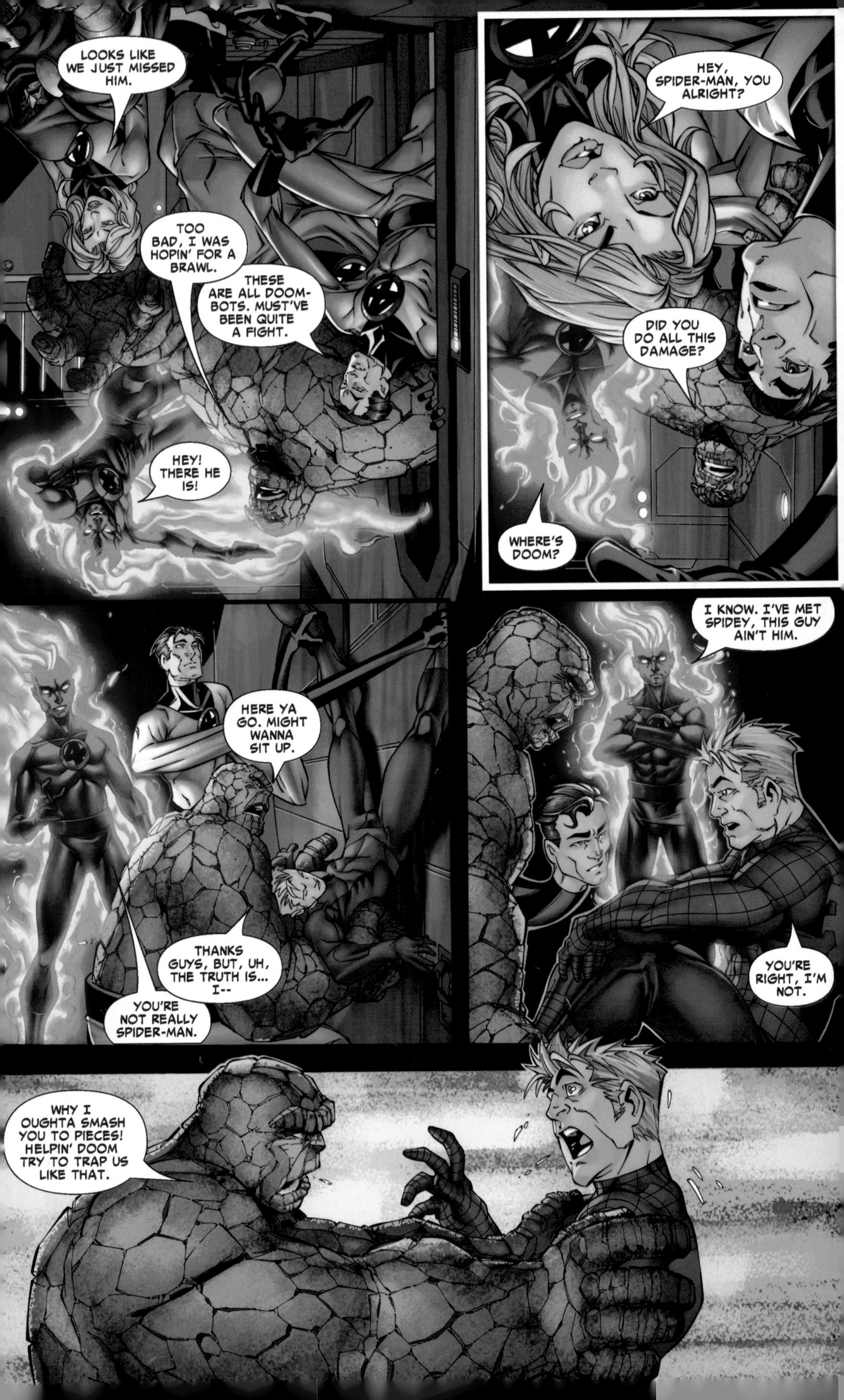
LOOKS LIKE WE JUST MISSED HIM.
TOO BAD, I WAS HOPIN' FOR A BRAWL.
THESE ARE ALL DOOM-BOTS. MUST'VE BEEN QUITE A FIGHT.
HEY! THERE HE IS!
HEY, SPIDER-MAN, YOU ALRIGHT?
DID YOU DO ALL THIS DAMAGE?
WHERE'S DOOM?
HERE YA GO. MIGHT WANNA SIT UP.
THANKS GUYS, BUT, UH, THE TRUTH IS... I--
YOU'RE NOT REALLY SPIDER-MAN.
I KNOW. I'VE MET SPIDEY, THIS GUY AIN'T HIM.
YOU'RE RIGHT, I'M NOT.
WHY I OUGHTA SMASH YOU TO PIECES! HELPIN' DOOM TRY TO TRAP US LIKE THAT.

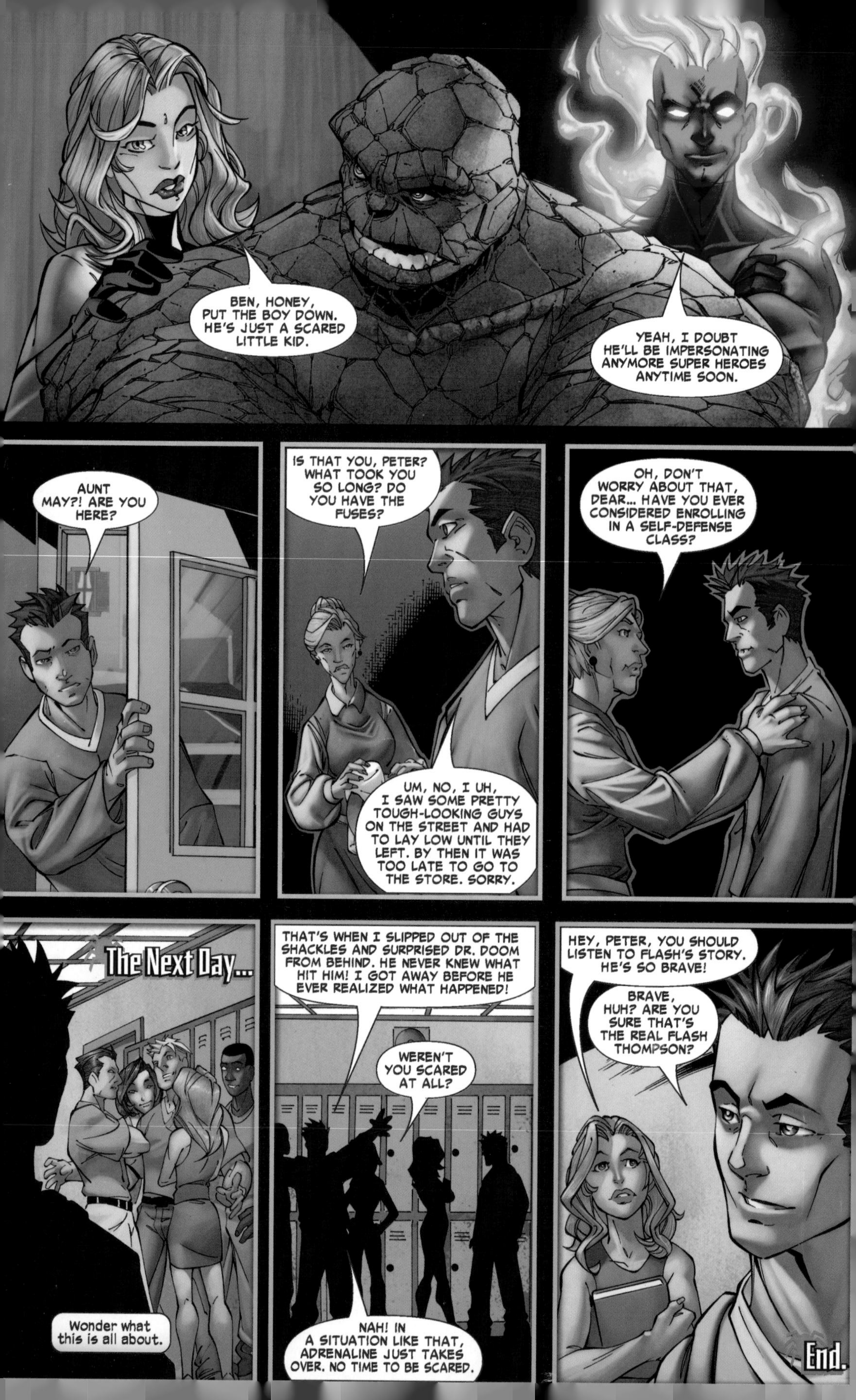
BEN, HONEY, PUT THE BOY DOWN. HE'S JUST A SCARED LITTLE KID.
YEAH, I DOUBT HE'LL BE IMPERSONATING ANYMORE SUPER HEROES ANYTIME SOON.
AUNT MAY?! ARE YOU HERE?
IS THAT YOU, PETER? WHAT TOOK YOU SO LONG? DO YOU HAVE THE FUSES?
UM, NO, I UH, I SAW SOME PRETTY TOUGH-LOOKING GUYS ON THE STREET AND HAD TO LAY LOW UNTIL THEY LEFT. BY THEN IT WAS TOO LATE TO GO TO THE STORE. SORRY.
OH, DON'T WORRY ABOUT THAT, DEAR... HAVE YOU EVER CONSIDERED ENROLLING IN A SELF-DEFENSE CLASS?
The Next Day...
Wonder what this is all about.
THAT'S WHEN I SLIPPED OUT OF THE SHACKLES AND SURPRISED DR. DOOM FROM BEHIND. HE NEVER KNEW WHAT HIT HIM! I GOT AWAY BEFORE HE EVER REALIZED WHAT HAPPENED!
WEREN'T YOU SCARED AT ALL?
NAH! IN A SITUATION LIKE THAT, ADRENALINE JUST TAKES OVER. NO TIME TO BE SCARED.
HEY, PETER, YOU SHOULD LISTEN TO FLASH'S STORY. HE'S SO BRAVE!
BRAVE, HUH? ARE YOU SURE THAT'S THE REAL FLASH THOMPSON?
End.